the Pinkaboos

BITTERLY AND THE GIANT PROBLEM

For Molly. The bravest little girl we know.
—JG & LG

For Jane and Lilly.
—BK

Other Books by Jake Gosselin and Laura Gosselin

*The Pinkaboos: Belladonna
and the Nightmare Academy*

BITTERLY AND THE GIANT PROBLEM

Jake Gosselin and Laura Gosselin

Illustrated by Billy Kelly

Andrews McMeel Publishing®

a division of Andrews McMeel Universal

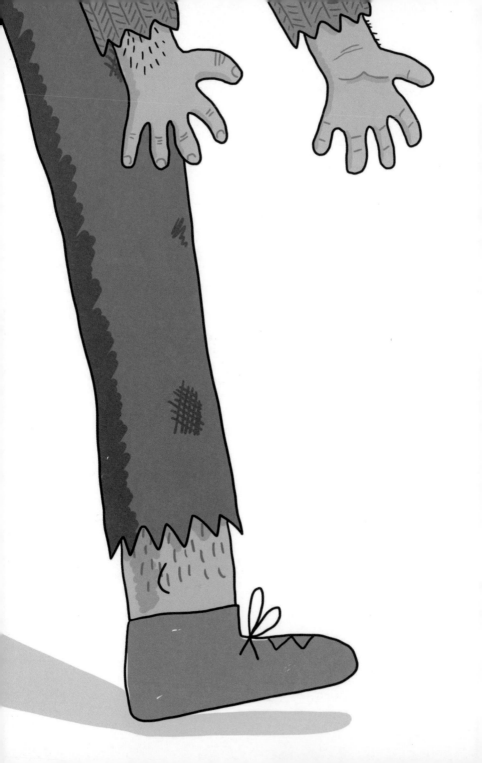

PROLOGUE

☠ ☠ ☠

Molly pedaled faster than she had ever pedaled before. Sweat beaded on her forehead. The giant was after her again.

He lumbered behind her, cracked lips snarling around a broken set of yellow teeth, filthy tattered rags for clothes. His club, an uprooted oak tree, hung menacingly over his shoulder. Fear grabbed hold of Molly and sent her pedaling with a new boost of energy.

The giant was slow, but his strides were long, and he was catching up fast. Molly ditched her bike, ran behind a tree, and held her breath. Her hands were shaking as she clasped them together.

She could feel the giant looking for her, shaking the earth with every powerful movement. He picked up a large rock nearby, looked beneath it, then threw it back down. Molly started to climb the tree she was hiding behind. She was good at climbing trees, even though her mom and dad warned her not to. She put one leg up on a branch and hoisted herself up, keeping an eye on the giant, who had begun pulling apart some bushes behind her. Molly reached for another branch and pulled herself up more. She angled her foot onto yet a higher, thinner branch, which made a loud snapping noise when she put weight on it. She stopped. She held her breath and turned to look at the giant.

The giant had stopped looking in the bush. Molly's heart sank as she realized his eyes were locked on her.

"You be lunch!" he boomed. Molly tried to scramble down the tree as fast as she could, but she

only got tangled in the leaves and twigs.

The giant lurched forward and before she knew it, he was standing at the bottom of the tree. Molly froze. The giant squatted, put his arms around each side of the trunk, and, with a mighty heave, pulled the tree up, roots and all.

Molly felt herself rising into the sky. She hung on as best she could, then lost her footing and began dangling helplessly from a branch as the giant held the tree up over his head.

"Noooooo!" Molly yelled. "Help! Somebody help me!"

Far, far away, in the Land of the Frights, a viper slept in her cool, damp cave. She slithered from side to side and hissed in her sleep. She could hear Molly's cries, and she woke with a start.

"Another little girl needs our help," she said to herself.

I t was a crisp autumn afternoon in the Land of the Frights. Three best friends, Bitterly, Belladonna, and Abyssma, were walking together to Fright School.

"I had a dream last night," said Abyssma. "And in the dream I met my little girl. She was beautiful, with big horns and little arms, and the whitest row of teeth."

"Little girls don't have horns!" said Belladonna.

"How do you know?" asked Abyssma. "Have you seen *all* the little girls?"

Abyssma had horns. She thought they looked lovely and believed every little girl could benefit from a set of her own.

"There has been no record of a little girl with horns," Belladonna said matter-of-factly over the rim of her glasses at Abyssma.

"If a little girl did have horns, it would be mentioned in a book," Belladonna added. Belladonna believed all things worth knowing could be found in books, while Bitterly thought the world was a little more complicated. Bitterly had spent a great deal of her time learning about little girls because the most important thing to every fright was to help her little girl. This wouldn't happen until the fright was ready, of course, and it would be the culmination of years of studying at Fright School.

Of the three friends, Bitterly worried the most. She worried she would never be good enough to even meet her little girl, let alone help her. Her magic powers had never been tested, and she wasn't sure what made her scary enough to be a good fright. She knew her teacher, Miss Viper, had confidence in her, but she didn't really know why. And Bitterly had other worries, too. . . .

Bitterly felt something hit her in the back of her head. She turned around to see Abyssma grinning at her. Abyssma had pelted an acorn at her.

"Oh, it is *on*," Bitterly said, laughing as she reached down and grabbed several acorns of her own. In a matter of seconds all three frights were hurling acorns at each other as hard as they could. Bitterly accidentally let one fly right at Belladonna's face.

"*Braxensheffanegg!*" Belladonna shouted as she swiped one of her hands downward. A force field appeared around her, and the acorn bounced off it and landed on the ground in front of the stunned frights.

"Whoa," Abyssma gasped. "That was so, so, so cool!"

"Cool is right!" murmured Bitterly. "How did you do that?"

Belladonna looked just as startled. She glanced at her hands. "I've been memorizing some basic spells from my spellbook," she admitted. "I can't believe it actually worked!" Belladonna paused, picked up the acorn, and examined it. "Please don't tell Miss Viper," she whispered, looking up at her friends.

"Don't worry," Abyssma, said, grinning. "Just don't forget to give us some tips when we start practicing."

💀 💀 💀

The frights continued down the path toward school. Abyssma and Belladonna walked quickly toward the spindly black iron gates of Fright School. Bitterly's pace slowed to a shuffle, and she began to trail behind Abyssma and Belladonna. Her head slunk down as leaves swirled at her feet. She knew what was coming.

"C'mon, Bitterly!" Abyssma yelled behind her.

"I'm coming," Bitterly mumbled. Bitterly looked up. She saw her two best friends walking briskly ahead of her. They were such sweet and wonderful frights. It made Bitterly sad that anyone could ever be mean to them. Beyond them, Bitterly could see the outlines of three more frights. They were there every day. A tall one with two shorter ones leaned against the gates, waiting.

Belladonna grabbed Bitterly's hand. "Don't worry about Vex," she said. "I read a book about bullies. Vex is worried she's not good enough, so she picks on people smaller than her."

"I know," Bitterly muttered.

As they approached, Vex, the tallest of the three, ran in front of the gate to block them.

"Look what the bat dragged in," Vex sneered. Her two friends laughed.

"C'mon. Let us by," Belladonna said.

"You know the password," Vex said.

"You're not very nice!" Abyssma yelled, her horns turning bright red.

"That's true," Vex smiled, "but that's not the password."

Bitterly swallowed hard and cleared her throat. She had been thinking about this speech for a while, and she just needed to summon the courage to give it. Every night, Bitterly lay awake thinking about what she would one day say to Vex to make her change her ways. She had written and rewritten the speech in her mind many times. Was now the time to give it? Bitterly cleared her throat.

"V—Vex," she stammered.

"Wha—What?" Vex mocked. "Come on, Bitterly, it's just one little word."

"Vex, we will not say the password," Bitterly announced.

"What password?" Vex asked.

"Pinkaboo," Bitterly answered.

"Aha! You said it. You may enter." Vex laughed and stepped aside.

Vex's friends doubled over with laughter. Looking defeated, Belladonna and Abyssma walked slowly through the gate. Bitterly looked down at her black shoes and followed sadly behind.

"The Pinkaboos" was what Vex called Bitterly, Abyssma, and Belladonna, and it had been spreading like wildfire around Fright School. It was a name Vex had made up to mean that they would never be able to scare. And in Fright School, a fright needed to be . . . well . . . frightening. Since Vex had begun her "Pinkaboo" campaign, Fright School had been a lot harder for Bitterly. When she and her friends walked the halls, she could hear murmurings from fellow frights—frights who *used* to be her friends—and classmates stopped saying hello to her in the hallways, instead whispering the word "Pinkaboo" as she passed by. That name tapped into what Bitterly feared most in the world—not being a good fright and never being able to help a little girl.

CHAPTER 2

At the beginning of class, Miss Viper seemed excited. She cleared her throat and slithered to the middle of the room.

"My little frights," she began. "Today is a very important day; Bitterly will meet her little girl."

The class gasped.

"Holy poop!" Abyssma squealed as she squeezed Bitterly's arm.

Bitterly felt her tummy churn. This was the moment she had been waiting for her entire life, but now that it was finally here, she was scared.

"Now, Bitterly, I chose you first because I think you show promise, and there's a little girl who needs you."

A screen dropped down from the ceiling and an image of a little girl, sound asleep in her bedroom, appeared.

Miss Viper cleared her throat and said, "This is Molly."

"Awwww," the frights chorused.

Molly had her sheets pulled up around her small face . . . but something was wrong. Her forehead was wrinkled with worry. She cried out and began tossing and turning in her bed, her sheets tangling in her arms as she flailed.

"Molly is afraid of a giant," Miss Viper announced.

The class broke out into laughter. "But giants are so adorable!" Abyssma laughed. "I just wanna squeeze 'em!"

"I've been teaching my pet giant to fetch!" another fright exclaimed.

"Class!" Miss Viper hissed. The laughing stopped. "As I've said before—human dreams are very

different from the fright world. What are adorable pets to us can be ferocious monsters to humans."

All the little frights exchanged surprised looks. How could little girls be afraid of such sweet, cuddly things as giants? Miss Viper turned and looked directly at Bitterly.

"Now one thing you must remember, Bitterly," she said. "I want you to be very careful in Molly's dream. You can teach your little girl to use her imagination in the dream world, but you may not, under any circumstances, use your magic, no matter how much you want to. As I've said before, the magic of a fright is powerful and unpredictable, especially in the wild dreams of children."

"Yes, Miss Viper," Bitterly said.

"Bitterly, your little girl is very scared and needs you desperately," Miss Viper said. "Go into her dream. Teach her."

And with that Miss Viper pulled a wand from thin air, waved it in a circle, and the screen opened up. Before Bitterly could say anything—before she could tell Miss Viper that she needed more time, that she didn't know if she could do it, and that she wondered if Molly could be assigned to another fright—before she could say anything at all, she was hoisted off her seat and sucked into the screen. With mouths hanging open, the little frights watched as Bitterly appeared on the screen. She was crouched in a corner of Molly's dream world; it was foggy and dark.

All the frights were transfixed by the screen.

One fright, Nettle, leaned over to her friend Oblivia and whispered, "I wonder how this is gonna go."

Oblivia giggled. "She's such a Pinkaboo. I bet she totally messes it up."

Abyssma turned around in her desk. With her horns blazing red, she shouted, "I'm gonna mess *you* up!"

Abyssma lurched forward and picked up Oblivia's desk with her teeth. The little fright screamed in horror as she clung to her desk, now held vertically by Abyssma's pointy teeth.

"Please, Abyssma," Oblivia squealed. "I was just joking."

"Abyssma!" Miss Viper snapped. "Put her down at once!"

Abyssma's horns turned from red to pale pink. She slowly let the desk down, placing it gently on the ground.

"Sorry, Miss Viper," Abyssma said solemnly.

"You must control your—"

Screaming cut off Miss Viper. She looked at the screen and saw Molly running away from a stumbling giant. Bitterly stood awkwardly as the little girl ran toward her.

"Come on, Bitterly," Miss Viper muttered under her breath. "Be the great fright I know you can be."

CHAPTER 3

💀 💀 💀

Suddenly, Bitterly found herself no longer in a classroom, but in a dark world where gloomy trees drooped sadly. A little girl was running toward her. It was Molly.

"Ahhhhhhhhhhh!" Molly screamed, dodging Bitterly as she went by.

Behind Molly was an angry giant. "You be lunch!" he boomed.

As he stomped by, Bitterly tapped him on his ankle and said: "Excuse me. Can you leave her alone? She's actually kind of scared of you, which is silly. . . ."

But unlike the nice giants she'd met before,

this one seemed completely uninterested in polite conversation, ignoring Bitterly entirely.

Running ahead and positioning herself between the giant and Molly, Bitterly held one hand up and shouted, "Attention, Mr. Giant!" But the giant marched right by her, his heavy strides causing the ground to rumble beneath her.

Bitterly thought about how all the frights in her class would be watching this on the screen. She thought about how some of the frights would be laughing at her right now. They might even be calling her a Pinkaboo. That's when she knew she had to do something quick.

Bitterly ran and caught up with Molly. She ran beside her until Molly noticed her.

"Who are you?" Molly yelled.

"I'm Bitterly."

"What are you doing here?" Molly yelled back.

"Running beside you," Bitterly replied.

"Are you scared, too? I feel like I'm never going to get away from him!" Molly yelled.

"He doesn't scare me," Bitterly said. "He's kind of funny if you think about it."

"Funny?" Molly screamed back.

"Well, he does have one of the biggest butts I've ever seen," Bitterly said, giggling.

Molly didn't laugh. She began to run even faster.

If Bitterly could just use her magic, this would be so much easier. "Do you have a banana?" Bitterly asked.

"A what?" Molly screamed.

"A banana!"

"How can you think of food at a time like this?" Molly cried. "He's going to eat *us* for lunch!"

"Just trust me on this," Bitterly pleaded. "Imagine a banana is in your hand."

Molly looked at Bitterly like she had no idea what was going on, but something inside her was tired of being scared; she wanted to try something new. Bitterly gave her a nod of encouragement, and Molly quickly closed her eyes and thought for a second. When she opened her eyes, she held out her hand. She was holding a banana.

"Great!" Bitterly shouted as she snatched the banana, peeled it, and began to eat.

"I don't know who you are, but you're crazy!" Molly yelled to Bitterly.

Bitterly finished the last bite, wiped her face, and flashing a mischievous grin said, "Watch this!" She turned and threw the peel onto the ground. As the giant approached, he slipped and fell with a massive crash.

Both girls turned around to see the helpless giant flailing on the ground. Bitterly began to laugh. And for the first time, Molly began to smile.

"Something's weird," Molly said. She shook her head back and forth and then asked, "Is this . . . a dream?"

Suddenly, Bitterly was sucked out of the dark world and into her classroom seat. She was back in Miss Viper's room. All the frights' eyes were on her.

"Whoa," she whispered.

CHAPTER 4

After class all the little frights hopped and fluttered their way to the door, but before Bitterly could leave, Miss Viper stuck her tail in front of her. "Stay a minute, Bitterly," Miss Viper said. "I'd like to speak with you."

"I'll meet up with you guys outside," Bitterly called to her friends before turning back to Miss Viper. "Sure thing, Miss Viper."

"Bitterly, what do you think the hardest part of being a fright is?" Miss Viper asked.

"Helping our little girls, I guess," Bitterly said.

"That's what we do . . . but why is that so difficult?" Miss Viper asked as she slithered around the room.

"I don't know. I guess once people are afraid of something, it's hard to get them to stop."

"Exactly!" Miss Viper exclaimed. "Fear is a very powerful thing because it sticks around if you don't learn how to face it."

The screen dropped down, and Molly appeared again.

"Have a seat, Bitterly."

Bitterly slunk down in her chair and looked up at the screen. Molly was awake now, sitting up in bed, lost in thought. Perhaps she was thinking about her dream; perhaps she was thinking about Bitterly. Maybe she was thinking about how silly the giant had looked lying on the ground.

"I expected more from you, Bitterly," Miss Viper said. "This isn't comedy hour. Throwing a banana peel was a cheap trick that worked in the moment, but it isn't going to help Molly face her fears in the long run."

Bitterly felt her eyes well up with tears. "What can I do to help her?"

Miss Viper pulled a remote out of thin air and began changing the channels on the screen.

"Let me show you something, Bitterly," she said.

The channels flicked from zombies to mummies and stopped on witches flying on broomsticks. The witches cackled in the way that witches do—high-pitched and menacing—as they darted around trees and careened over rooftops. A light in one of the houses caught Bitterly's attention. Inside, an old woman with big blue eyes looked out.

The witches headed toward the house, shrieking and whooping with horrid delight. They flew up to the window, hovering their broomsticks in midair in front of it and scratching at it with their long, curled yellow nails.

"We've come for you!" one witch screeched.

The woman on the other side of the window smiled back at them.

"She's not afraid of witches?" Bitterly asked.

"No," Miss Viper said proudly. "But she used to be."

The woman held out her hand and showed the witch a set of keys.

The witch screamed in terror and pounded on her broomstick with her fist. "Go, go, go!"

The broomstick began to fly chaotically, smacking into a lamppost while the witch clung on helplessly.

The woman then pushed a button on the keys, and a car alarm began blaring.

BEEP-BEEP-BEEP-BEEP-BEEP-BEEP. WEEEEOOOO-WEEEEOOOO-WEEEE-OOOO. ANNT-ANNT-ANNT-ANNT.

Two witches immediately fell off their broomsticks and landed in the trees below. One terrified witch began flying in circles while another sobbed hysterically. With wide eyes, Bitterly watched the woman, who calmly observed the witches from her window.

"Who is she?" Bitterly murmured in awe.

"She was my little girl . . . all grown up now," Miss Viper said softly.

"How did she know to do that?" Bitterly said.

"Witches are afraid of loud noises," Miss Viper said. "I taught her how to scare them."

Miss Viper pressed a button on the remote, and the channel turned back to Molly, who had switched on the lamp beside her bed.

"Molly's bad dreams are making her afraid of the dark," Miss Viper said. "Pretty soon she won't want to go to bed at all."

"But how do I teach Molly to scare the giant?"

"Teach her to *be* the fear. She can *become* the darkness!" Miss Viper said.

With that, she pulled a wand from nowhere, touched the top of her scaly head, and vanished, leaving Bitterly alone in the classroom.

CHAPTER 5

That night as Bitterly went to sleep in her shiny black coffin—one of the soft, cozy rectangular beds all little frights slept in—she could see her reflection in the paint as she lay awake.

Inside each coffin were murals that represented the unique strengths of each fright. Bitterly's showed a pink moon above a shining sea. She wasn't sure what it meant, but she had a feeling she'd understand in time. Bitterly nervously bit her lip trying to make sense of everything. She thought about Miss Viper's advice. What had she meant about becoming the darkness?

If Molly was afraid of the dark, how could becoming the darkness make her any less scared?

She closed her eyes tight and began hearing Vex's taunting voice in her head.

"Pinkaboo!"

She rolled over and tried to sleep on her side.

"Pinkaboo! Pinkaboo! Pinkaboo!"

Bitterly groaned and rolled over on her other side.

She kept thinking about Vex, the darkness, and little Molly's giant . . . and then . . . everything went black.

Bitterly was suddenly walking beside a foggy lake. She looked over, and Vex was walking beside her.

"You're nothing but a Pinkaboo," Vex said, laughing.

"Why won't you stop?" Bitterly pleaded.

"I'm only doing this because I can," Vex said.

"What does that mean?" Bitterly said.

Suddenly Molly stepped out of the fog. "It means as long as you're not sure of yourself, Vex has power over you," she said.

"Molly!" Bitterly exclaimed. "What are you doing here?"

"Hey, you came into my dream—I thought it was only fair if I came into yours." Molly smiled. "Hold my hand."

Bitterly reached over and joined hands with Molly.

Vex jumped in front of both of them shouting, "Pinkaboo!"

"Start walking," Molly insisted.

"Pinkaboo!" Vex cackled. "You silly, silly Pinkaboo!"

"Don't let yourself feel anything bad," Molly whispered to Bitterly. "Don't let yourself feel sadness or hurt or embarrassment. Just feel pride."

Molly clutched Bitterly's hand tighter. They walked for what seemed like miles as Vex continued to taunt them. She was relentless. Her wings stretched out as she swirled around them, dancing and yelling "Pinkaboo!" at the top of her lungs.

Vex began throwing magic fireballs at them.
Worried about such a reckless use of magic,
Bitterly imagined a baseball glove. Suddenly one
appeared on Molly's hand as well as her own. They
began catching the fireballs and throwing them
back at Vex.

"This feels good!" Bitterly finally smiled.

"Yes!" Molly said.

"In fact, it feels better than good!" Bitterly said,
looking directly at Vex. Vex's wicked grin slowly

faded into a drooping frown as she dodged and
hurled fireballs.

Bitterly had never seen Vex anything but angry
and mean. Seeing her sad was very strange.

"Don't take away my power," she whimpered.

Molly smiled at Bitterly. "Do it, Bitterly," Molly
said. "Be a Pinkaboo!"

"What?" Bitterly said.

"Be a Pinkaboo! Be a Pinkaboo! Be a Pinkaboo!"

"Stop it!" Vex yelled angrily. "Stop it both of you!"

Bitterly awoke with a start.

"That's it," she said aloud to herself. "I'm gonna
be a Pinkaboo!"

CHAPTER 6

♥♥♥

Even though Bitterly was late for school and running so hard that her legs hurt, she couldn't help but smile. She knew how to help Molly!

She turned the corner going full speed and ran right into Vex. Bitterly's books went flying, papers were lost to the wind, and pencils rolled off the edge of the sidewalk into the gutter. Bitterly looked up from where she'd landed on the pavement, and Vex grinned a mean grin.

"Well, well, well. If it isn't a little Pinkaboo. That wasn't very nice, little Pinkaboo. Hitting me like that."

"It was an accident, Vex, and you know it!"

"Oh, are you going to tell me what I know now? I don't think so, Pinkaboo."

"Keep trying to intimidate me, Vex," Bitterly said. "It won't work anymore. You're more scared than all the little girls put together!"

Vex cackled outrageously.

"Well, look at this—we're not on school grounds." Vex pointed at the edge of the schoolyard a block away. "And you know what that means . . ."

Vex's wings spread as she began casting a spell. Bitterly recognized it immediately; it was called the

Goo Blast. She had read about it in Belladonna's *Big Book of Blasts* and knew it could badly hurt a fright, so she had to do something quick.

Vex's hands twisted and wiggled in that way they do when a fright casts a spell. A sickly green light started to glow all around Vex as she spoke louder and louder in the mind-bending language of magic.

"Just a little Pinkaboo. Nobody is going to miss you," Vex sneered between chants.

Bitterly had no choice. She didn't know what her powers could do, but she had to try. She had to cast something.

"Hey, everybody, Bitterly is fighting Vex!" Abyssma shouted from the schoolyard. Soon, Vex and Bitterly were surrounded by a chorus of frights chanting, "Fight! Fight! Fight!" Vex's voice raised in a crescendo as she finished her spell, releasing the blast from her outstretched hand.

Just like an acorn, Bitterly thought as she quickly realized what she had to do.

"Braxensheffanegg!" she shouted while waving her hand downward, just like she had seen Belladonna do.

The magic force shield sprang up around Bitterly just before the goo blast hit her. Vex's eyes widened in surprise as the sickly green slime slammed into the shield before the barrier shuddered, cracked, and then exploded into pieces. The defense spell had blocked the goo blast, but the force of the spell was enough to knock Bitterly backward into a tree.

Vex approached, already starting to conjure a second attack.

Bitterly did not know powerful blast spells like Vex did, but she remembered a couple more things from Belladonna's spellbook.

"*Sheethoslappo!*" Bitterly commanded, and a little black cloud appeared in front of Vex. It immediately started to rain, forming a puddle at Vex's feet.

Vex's confusion quickly turned to laughter. "What are you going to do, Pinkaboo? Rain on my victory parade?" she asked as she stepped into the puddle and continued casting her spell.

"No," Bitterly said, breathing hard. "I expect you to fall. *Flashcoballichill!*" Bitterly shouted as she spread her arms out to either side like she was quickly parting some invisible curtains.

The puddle that Vex was standing in suddenly turned to ice, causing her to slip and fall hard on her back.

Seeing her chance to escape, Bitterly jumped up and bolted for the school grounds. The frights who'd circled them parted and cheered as she raced away.

Vex shot up off the ground and chased after Bitterly, running faster than Bitterly had ever seen any fright run. Vex was catching up to her, and

Bitterly realized she wasn't going to make it to the school grounds in time. The frights who had been watching the fight were following them both.

Vex caught up with Bitterly just before the school gates and grabbed her arm. With everyone watching, Bitterly turned to face Vex. She looked

right into her black eyes and said, "I'm a Pinkaboo, and I'm proud of it!"

"What?" Vex laughed.

"I'm a PINKABOOOOOOO!" Bitterly shouted.

A collective gasp resounded among the little frights.

Belladonna ran over and stood behind Bitterly.

"Yeah, I'm a Pinkaboo, too!" she announced, adjusting her glasses.

"Me, too!" Abyssma's voice squealed from the crowd of frights, the top tips of her horns sticking out.

Vex looked around at all the little eyes staring at her. "Well . . . well, that means you're . . . you're weak!" Vex stammered.

"Why are we weak?" Bitterly calmly asked.

Vex took a step back. "You just are!" she yelled.

"OK. We're weak," Bitterly said. "So what? We're all weak in some way or another . . . and so are our little girls. But isn't that why we're all here, to learn how to face fear? Because . . . well, after all, fear is just weakness."

Bitterly swallowed hard, took a few steps forward, and got very close to Vex's face.

"I am glad I'm weak. It means . . . um . . . well, I guess it means I'm in the right place. I'm here to learn how to . . . how to overcome it," Bitterly

said, beginning to realize it herself. She smiled, looked Vex straight in the eye, and announced, "I'm a Pinkaboo, and I'm proud of it."

She raised her arms and looked around the crowd of her fellow frights. "We are all Pinkaboos!" she yelled triumphantly.

CHAPTER 7

There was a hum of excitement in Miss Viper's class that day. Everyone was talking about what had happened between Vex and Bitterly. Bitterly got lots of high-fives from other frights, many of whom confessed that they'd been afraid of Vex, too.

"Class," Miss Viper hissed, "settle down!"

"Yes, Miss Viper," the frights replied in unison.

"Now, today is a very special day. As you all know, Bitterly is going to go back into Molly's dream, and we get to watch again. This will prepare you all for when you meet your little girls."

She slithered over to Bitterly's desk. "Now, Bitterly, remember what we talked about?" Miss Viper asked.

"I dreamed about it," Bitterly replied.

"Good—that's good," Miss Viper said as she pulled the screen down. The image of Molly sleeping appeared on the screen.

"Awwww," everyone cooed once again.

"Now. Go." Miss Viper waved her wand. Before she knew it, Bitterly was sucked into the screen, and she was once again running beside Molly.

"You again?" Molly said as she ran through a creepy forest lit by nothing more than a thin sliver of moon.

"Looks like we're in this together for the long haul," said Bitterly, smiling and looking behind her. The same giant was chasing them.

"The giant again?" Bitterly asked.

"I just can't shake him!" Molly shouted. The giant's heavy steps shook the earth.

He was getting closer. They could hear him laughing—a low rumble, like an avalanche in his chest.

"I have a plan," she said. "We're going to scare him away."

"What? How?" Molly asked nervously.

"We need to make it dark," Bitterly said. "The moon is too bright. Imagine a huge blanket covering it."

"Are you kidding?" Molly yelled. "I'm afraid of the dark!"

"Yes, I know," Bitterly replied, grinning. "But I know a few things about giants."

"I'm too scared," Molly moaned.

"It's your dream. Remember, you can create anything," Bitterly said as she looked up at the approaching giant. "And you might want to do it soon."

Molly took a deep breath. "OK, I'll give it a try," she said as she closed her eyes and focused.

"Good," Bitterly whispered. "Now . . . it's *his* turn to be afraid."

Suddenly an enormous pink blanket floated down over the moon and plunged the dream into darkness. The girls stopped running.

"Now I'm really scared," Molly whispered.

"You don't have to be scared if you don't want to be," Bitterly insisted. "Have you noticed how you can't hear the giant anymore? He's not moving because he's scared, too."

"So *he's* afraid of the dark?" Molly asked.

"All giants are," Bitterly said.

"Good," Molly said. She closed her eyes and focused once again. This time when she opened them, she could see.

Molly had imagined a pair of night-vision goggles for each of them. They now saw the dream world in perfect clarity through the goggles' green lenses and turned back to face the giant.

Bitterly blinked behind her goggles in surprise. "Great idea, Molly!"

Standing before them, the giant looked very worried. He was searching for something.

Slowly they crept behind the giant, who was frantically pulling things out of his pockets: a red truck, a moose, and an oven all fell heavily to the ground at his feet.

Bitterly led Molly as they scurried up into a tree. There they sat and watched as the giant fished out a box of giant-size matches from his back pocket.

Molly noticed how the darkness didn't seem scary anymore; it felt like a blanket that she could hide under. It was fun to be the one sneaking around in the dark.

With the help of her goggles, Molly was able
to see that each match was a tree trunk with a red
tip on the end. The giant struck one of the matches
against the box, and a bright fiery flame lit up the
darkness.

"This not funny anymore," rumbled the giant as
he held the lit match nervously in front of his face.

Bitterly leaned over and whispered in Molly's
ear: "Look. The fear is sinking into him. His fears
will do all the work for us; we just need to give
them a little push."

Bitterly started to climb down the tree. When Molly went to follow, Bitterly held her hand up. "Wait here. I'm going to lure him over, and I want you to scare him when he gets here."

"Me? What?" Molly's voice cracked.

"You're safe, Molly. Trust me," Bitterly smiled. "*You* are the darkness now."

"Uh, uh, uh . . . OK," Molly stammered.

Bitterly ran up behind the giant and made the creepiest noise Molly had ever heard. It sounded like a creaky door in a haunted house on Halloween night.

The giant spun around and shouted, "What was that?"

Bitterly was so fast, she had moved before the giant could shine his light on her. Then his match went out.

"Oh no, oh no, oh no!" the giant whimpered as Molly watched him scramble to light another. But his hands were shaking so much, it took several tries before the giant was able to light the second match. Bitterly was near the tree where Molly was hiding when she let out the same noise again, only this time a little louder.

The giant whimpered when he heard it, and Molly almost felt a tiny bit bad for him.

He came toward the tree where Molly was waiting. He was looking at the ground, where he'd heard Bitterly's eerie sound coming from, so he didn't notice when he walked right by Molly, so close that she could almost reach out and touch his big hairy ear.

Molly was feeling so much less scared, she decided to have a little fun of her own. She thought of all the noises that frightened her at night and remembered how creepy the water pipes in her house sounded—like a ghostly gasp. She made the exact same noise right into his ear. As soon as he heard it, the giant froze in his tracks and slowly lifted up the match with a trembling hand to where Molly sat in the tree.

As Molly came into the ominous glow of the match, she looked the giant right in the eye and yelled, "Boo!" Then she blew out the match.

"AHHHH, MONSTER!" The giant screamed as he ran in the opposite direction. Molly began chasing him.

"I'm right behind you!" she teased.

"NOOOOOOO!" he wailed.

Bitterly chased after Molly, laughing. "Isn't this fun? He's afraid of you!"

Molly stopped and turned.

"I love this, Bitterly," she said, giggling. "Thank you."

"I'm glad," Bitterly said. "And thank you for coming into *my* dream."

"I did?" Molly said.

"Yeah, you really helped me with some stuff," Bitterly said.

"Hmm. I don't remember doing that, but you're welcome—wait. Is this a dream?" She shook her head back and forth. Suddenly, Bitterly was sucked out of the dream, shooting through the screen and landing behind her desk in Miss Viper's class. All of the other little frights were clapping and cheering. Miss Viper had her small hands clasped in pride.

"Now, *that's* how you become a fright," she smiled.

itterly was ecstatic after class, but even
so, she wanted to be alone. Belladonna
and Abyssma wanted to go out for slices
of insect pie to celebrate, but Bitterly wasn't in the
mood. She walked up on the side of a secluded hill
and looked out at the crescent moon. She wished
she could talk to Molly without having to enter her
dreams. She wondered if Molly had really appeared
in her dream at all, or was it just her imagination?
She heard someone climbing the hill behind her.
The grass ruffled; the leaves blew into the wind and
danced about in the sky. She saw a thin hand with
fingers like long strings of gray yarn grasp at the

grass at the top of the hill. Then a head appeared—
wisps of green hair waved in the breeze. It was Vex.

Bitterly was astonished when Vex sat down next
to her. Her wings, once triumphant and shimmering
silver, now seemed to hang withered at her side.

"I heard you did real good work with your little
girl," Vex said. "Everyone's talking about it."

"Uhhh, thanks," Bitterly said. The two frights
were quiet for a while. Both seemed to be deep in
thought as the moon hung between the trees. A
gust of wind blew through Bitterly's black hair. Vex
looked at Bitterly and smiled.

"I had a little girl once," Vex said, finally breaking the silence. "I was always in her dreams."

"Really?" Bitterly asked.

Vex's eyes narrowed. She watched a beetle scurry up a long blade of gray grass in front of her. She hoisted up her pitch-black shoe and quickly smashed it.

"I was once Miss Viper's favorite student, too. I got the first little girl in our class, just like you did. Everyone was excited to see what I could do. I was excited, too," she said wistfully.

"What happened?" Bitterly asked. Vex's mouth contorted into a strange grimace.

"My little girl was afraid of ghosts. In her dreams, ghosts would moan from her closet and under her bed. I tried to scare the ghosts away, but they just laughed at me."

Vex clenched her sharp teeth as she muttered, "Their hollow laughter made me so mad."

"What did you do?" Bitterly asked.

"I used my magic," Vex said.

Bitterly gasped. Every fright knew how dangerous it was to use magic inside of a dream.

"Nothing was working, so I thought I'd just cast a simple frost spell to freeze one of them," Vex admitted. "And I was right. It was fine at first, but then things went wrong. My spells got out of control and it was like . . . like I couldn't stop casting them. I started blasting the ghosts with fire and lightning. My hair stood on end, my teeth became sharper, and my wings . . . well, they used to look like butterfly wings."

She paused and a smile crept upon her face. "My little girl was more terrified than she'd ever been."

"That's awful." Bitterly put her hand on Vex's bony shoulder, but Vex shrugged her away and continued, "I became my little girl's nightmare. I would sometimes find myself in her dreams, and I was scaring her, not helping her."

"Holy bats!" Bitterly exclaimed. "We have to do something. Let's go talk to Miss Viper right now!"

Vex laughed. "Oh you silly little Pinkaboo. Don't you get it? This is what I was meant to do. I was never meant to be a silly fright; I was meant to be a nightmare."

The two frights let Vex's words hang in the air for a moment. Bitterly could feel her heart beating hard in her chest.

"I'm my little girl's nightmare, and now I'm yours, too," Vex murmured.

"No," Bitterly said. "You're . . . you're just confused. You used magic in a dream, and you shouldn't have, and maybe it did something to you, but . . . but you can be a fright again!"

"You don't get it, do you?" Vex said as she stood up. "I love being a nightmare."

Vex turned to fly away, and Bitterly shouted, "This isn't over, Vex!"

Vex hovered over Bitterly and glared. "You're right, my little Pinkaboo. It's only just beginning."

CHAPTER 9

☠ ☠ ☠

Miss Viper's class the next day was full of intense lessons. She taught the little frights how to put a dragon on a leash and that unraveling mummies can be a quick fix in a pinch. But most important, she wanted the frights to teach their little girls to be the fear themselves. This was the hardest part. Abyssma's horns turned red.

"Now, my frights, don't get too frustrated. One day you will have your magic to help you." Abyssma's horns turned back to pink polka dots, and she looked relieved.

"But . . ." Miss Viper continued, "I know some of you have already been experimenting with magic."

She shot a glance at Bitterly, who looked quickly down at her shoes.

"Magic is never to be used until you truly comprehend what your powers are. Understood?"

"Yes, Miss Viper," the class chorused back. Bitterly mumbled it quietly.

Just before the bell rang, Miss Viper's eyes gazed across the classroom as the frights chattered excitedly and waited to be excused. Miss Viper's small black eyes rested on Belladonna, who was staring back—pencil in hand—eager to take more notes.

When the bell rang, it was time for the frights to head to the cafeteria, where Miss Slugworthy

had made a giant vat of bone soup. Bone soup was prepared once a month and was considered a delicacy among the frights.

As the frights jumped up from their desks, Miss Viper called: "Don't forget to read chapter six of your textbook. There might be a pop quiz on how to tangle a zombie's legs coming up. Until next class, my little frights."

Then she slithered over to Belladonna. "Belladonna. Stay for a moment?"

Belladonna didn't flinch.

As the last fright flitted out of the room, Miss Viper shut the door and looked at Belladonna.

"I have some news," she said firmly. "You're next to meet your little girl."

Belladonna flew out of her chair, glasses falling off as she hugged Miss Viper as hard as she could.

"Oh, thank you, thank you, thank you!" she cried. "You won't regret—"

Miss Viper cut her off, "It's not an easy one, I'm afraid. It's complicated," she hissed.

"Oh. Well, I know I can handle anything, Miss Viper," Belladonna said. "If it's a fear of ghosts, I'll hit them with chapter twelve of Fearsky and Boocharm's *Identifying and Removing Non-Corporeal Entities!* If it's spiders, I'll go with chapters three through six from Dr. Acid's seminal text, *Zen and the Art of Squishing Bugs—*"

Miss Viper cut her off again, "Your little girl's name is Ava. That's all I can tell you for now. And I have a book for you to read; I don't think you've ever read it before."

"Never read it before?" Belladonna looked skeptical. "I find that highly unlikely."

Miss Viper slithered over to the bookshelf and selected a book. She handed it to Belladonna, who grabbed it like a child opening her first gift on Christmas morning.

"Read this tonight," she hissed. "We'll talk after our next class. You are excused."

Belladonna looked down at the book and read the title out loud. *When Frights Become Nightmares.*

Bitterly

Despite her extreme apprehension about her own abilities, Bitterly is one of the most promising students in Fright School. Bitterly was the first of her class to be assigned a little girl to protect. Naturally gifted, Bitterly has the potential to do great things, but she'll need to overcome her own fears first.

Belladonna

The only thing Belladonna loves more than a good book is her friends. Driven to learn as much as she can, Belladonna spends most of her free time studying. She can recite any spell in a pinch and is very eager to help her first little girl overcome nightmares.

Abyssma

Abyssma is strong, independent, and fiercely loyal to her fellow Pinkaboos. She has a fabulous set of horns that change color when she's mad. They're pretty cool. Because she's the biggest Pinkaboo, bullies tend to keep their distance when she's around.

the
MAJOR FRIGHTS

Vex

Bullies are usually mean because they're not happy . . . and Vex is the school bully. To make herself feel better, Vex makes the younger frights feel bad about themselves by calling them names. She targets Bitterly and her friends, and Bitterly quickly learns that standing up to her isn't easy!

the
MAJOR FRIGHTS

Miss Viper

Miss Viper is the one and only teacher at Fright School. Since becoming a teacher in the year 1892 (which was a very long time ago), Miss Viper has taught young frights at Fright School how to enter the dreams of little girls to battle their nightmares.

MORE TO EXPLORE!

FUN FACTS and THINGS to MAKE!

Write Your Own Spooky Story!

If you have something that worries you at night, write a story about it! Make the story silly, and you'll see in no time that you will be less afraid of your fear! Are you afraid of ghosts? Give your ghost a silly name such as "Whooshy" and illustrate your story with cool pictures. Draw a silly hat on Whooshy. In no time, you'll find the ghost is less scary and more fun!

the SCIENCE of FEAR

Do you ever get scared in bed at night? When the lights go out, does your imagination run wild with spooky thoughts? Pinkafans, that's OK—and totally normal! Scientists have been studying fear for many years.

Here's what happens to your body when you're afraid:

* To keep you safe, your brain is always on the lookout for danger. If it senses trouble, your brain sends an alert to your body.

- Before you know it, your heart starts beating loud and fast.
- Your breathing changes, and you often begin sweating.
- In an instant, you may have a "fight or flight" reaction. This means your instincts tell you to stick around and fight whatever you're up against, or run away as fast as you can.

So why does fear exist? Fear helps us to detect danger. A long time ago, fear was a normal part of everyday life because people didn't have the stuff we have today that keeps us safe, such as fire engines and police officers. Sometimes, people would find themselves running away from grizzly bears or the hot lava from volcanoes! People relied on fear to help to keep them alert to all the things that could hurt them. We may not have the same dangers as our ancestors, but we can still have a similar reaction.

Bitterly's Advice on Getting Over Fears

So what's a good way to get over your fear? Bitterly says that facing your fear slowly will often help you to feel less afraid. Another good way is to talk about your fears with your parents, brothers, sisters, or friends. Talking about it can help you figure out why things are scary to you and sometimes change the way you think about them. You might find that once you figure out *why* something is scary, it diffuses the fear. "Diffuse" is just a fancy word for disappear, so once the fear disappears, you're not scared any more. Plus, it just feels good to find out that other people can be scared of things, too!

P.S. Bitterly says sometimes fear can be fun. If you like watching a scary movie, reading a spine-tingling book, or going on a roller coaster, then you have learned to have fun with fear.

GETTING OVER FEARS

the HISTORY of GIANTS

In *Bitterly and the Giant Problem*, we read about how Molly had a fear of giants that Bitterly helped her overcome. But where did the idea of giants come from? Here are some cool facts about giants:

* Almost every group of people in the world has stories they tell about giants, from the mighty Cyclops of Greek mythology to the frightful frost giants of Norse mythology—and even English fairy tales, such as "Jack and the Beanstalk."

* Giants come in many different shapes and sizes. Cyclops was a ferocious giant with just one eye and could throw huge rocks. The giant Atlas was big enough to carry the whole planet on his back!

* Frost giants often fought with gods like Thor. They could be very scary and sometimes had extra heads or arms. Some of them even looked like animals, like Fenrir the giant wolf!

* Paul Bunyan was a giant lumberjack. He was an unusual giant because he was not a bad guy. He was a hero! Many of his adventures focused on his incredible size and strength as he traveled the United States with his giant blue ox named Babe.

* Are giants real? Not the kinds that are in these old stories, but some people can grow to be quite tall. The tallest person in the world was named Robert Wadlow, and he was almost nine feet tall. If you stood on top of your own head, you still might not be as tall as him!

Make Your Own
"WORMY" CUPCAKES!

You will need:

* A box of chocolate cupcake mix
* Chocolate frosting (from scratch or store bought)
* Oreos
* Gummy worms and plastic spiders
* Help from a grown-up (if needed)

Steps:

1. Follow the directions on the cupcake box to make and bake your cupcakes. (You may need a grown-up to take things out of the hot oven.)

2. The fun part—smash your Oreos into tiny crumbs! This will be the "dirt." Put the crumbs in a bowl.

3. Frost your cupcakes with chocolate frosting.

4. Dip your chocolate cupcakes into the Oreo dirt.

5. Top with gummy worms and plastic spiders. Yummy!

About the Authors

Jake Gosselin grew up in Canada, where he spent his youth battling frost giants, tricking evil spirits, and talking to wolves. None of this can be proven, but it should be noted that a frost giant hasn't been seen since 1982.

As a child, Jake had numerous fears, including but not limited to zombies, vampires, ghosts, demons, gelatinous cubes, goblins, large insects, small insects, biting insects, horses, geese, monkeys, grouchy adults, and Brussels sprouts.

Now that Jake is an "adult," all of his fears are crammed into a deep corner of his mind. Occasionally he lets them out to play and writes down what he sees, which apparently makes him a writer. He lives in California with his wife, Laura; daughter, Molly; bearded dragon, Dezi; cat, Mittens; hamster, Peanut; and dog, Chewbacca.

Laura Gosselin grew up in England and used to stare out her classroom window so much that her teachers called her a daydreamer. Little did they know she was thinking up fun stories she could tell one day. Or perhaps she was sleeping with her eyes open.

When she was little, Laura was afraid of sharks in swimming pools and large bugs with wings. Now that she's a grown-up, Laura is afraid of laundry, bills, and whiny children. She is also super afraid of spiders. The bigger and hairier they are, the louder she screams.

After going to school in New York, living in Canada, and finally settling in Southern California, Laura has come to realize that only three things in life really matter: 1) happiness; 2) happiness; and finally, after much consideration, 3) happiness.

About the Illustrator

A 1993 graduate of the Cooper Union for the Advancement of Science and Art, Billy Kelly has been designing children's books since before you were born, if you were born after 1993.

In 2004, Billy and his wife, Jacqueline, launched their very own design studio, YAY! Design, in Lewisburg, Pennsylvania, and there was much rejoicing.

Since 2009, Billy has been writing and recording songs for kids. National Public Radio has praised Billy's quirky children's music for its "endearingly oddball sense of humor." His songs can be heard on SiriusXM Satellite Radio and on radio stations all across the land, assuming you have the radio turned on and tuned in to the right station at the exact right time. Billy was nominated for a 2016 Grammy for *Trees*, a children's album he recorded with South Carolina songwriter Molly Ledford. Oh—he is a stand-up comedian, too!

Be sure to check out the continuing adventures of Bitterly, Belladonna, and Abyssma in *The Pinkaboos: Belladonna and the Nightmare Academy!*

Andrews McMeel Publishing
a division of Andrews McMeel Universal
1130 Walnut Street, Kansas City, Missouri 64106
www.andrewsmcmeel.com

The Pinkaboos: Bitterly and the Giant Problem was first published in 2014, copyright
© 2014 by Robert Simon; Yay! Design, LLC; and L & G Creative Resources, Inc.,
dba SupperTime Entertainment. Illustrations copyright © 2014 by Billy Kelly. The
Pinkaboos concept and look was created by Gerry Renert, Billy Kelly, and Robert Simon.

16 17 18 19 20 SDB 10 9 8 7 6 5 4 3 2 1
ISBN: 978-1-4494-7831-5
Library of Congress Control Number: 2015959879

Made by:
Shenzhen Donnelley Printing Company Ltd.
Address and location of manufacturer:
No. 47, Wuhe Nan Road, Bantian Ind. Zone,
Shenzhen China, 518129
1st Printing—6/13/16

ATTENTION: SCHOOLS AND BUSINESSES
Andrews McMeel books are available at quantity discounts with bulk purchase
for educational, business, or sales promotional use. For information, please
e-mail the Andrews McMeel Publishing Special Sales Department:
specialsales@amuniversal.com.

Check out these and other books at ampkids.com

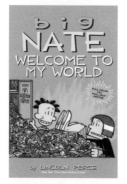

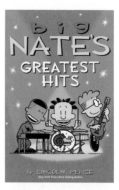

Also available:
Teaching and activity guides for each title.
AMP! Comics for Kids books make reading FUN!